To my Superhero Dad, with love
T.K.

For Mega-Matilda, Bionic-Bea and
Magic-Martha, from Dynamo-Dad x x x
J.B.

First published in 2015 by Nosy Crow Ltd,
The Crow's Nest, 10a Lant Street,
London SE1 1QR
www.nosycrow.com

ISBN 978 0 85763 168 8 (HB)
ISBN 978 0 85763 169 5 (PB)

Nosy Crow and associated logos are trademarks and/or registered trademarks of Nosy Crow Ltd.

Text copyright © Timothy Knapman 2015
Illustrations copyright © Joe Berger 2015

The right of Timothy Knapman to be identified as the author
of this work and of Joe Berger to be identified as the illustrator of this work has been asserted.

Printed in China
Papers used by Nosy Crow are made from wood grown in sustainable forests.

1 3 5 7 9 8 6 4 2 (HB)
1 3 5 7 9 8 6 4 2 (PB)

SUPERHERO DAD

TIMOTHY
KNAPMAN

illustrated by
JOE BERGER

Dads can be

quite ordinary,

but **mine's** not,
and I'm **glad**,

because,

you see,

he's secretly a . . .

HAM!

You can hear his **Super Snoring**

from a thousand miles away . . .

. . . so I jump up on his tummy shouting,

"Come on, Dad! It's day!"

He makes these
Super Breakfasts,
though he's only
half awake.

(So sometimes I'll get
toast with **chocolate**,
jam, ice cream
and **cake!**)

His jokes are
Super Funny . . .

. . . and his laugh is Super Long.

HA HA HA HA HA HA HA HA HA HA HA!

He can pick up
our dog Jumbo
so he must be
Super Strong.

Whenever we play dinosaurs, he does a . . .

oOoOoOOAR!

like this.
And afterwards he gives
me a Tyrannosaurus kiss.

When he **zooms**
me round and round,
I feel like
I can **fly.**

And when I'm on
his shoulders,
I am **taller**
than the **sky.**

He's very good
at woodwork, too
(you're MEANT to
bang your thumb).

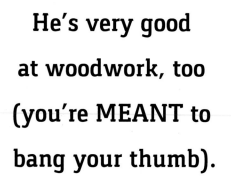

He **saws**
and **hammers,**
glues
and **paints,**
and makes the
wood become . . .

I call out "Dad!" but quietly
(the monsters mustn't hear) . . .

. . . and in he comes and,
just like that,
the monsters
disappear!

He holds me close and tells me that
there's something I should know.
"You're always, **always** safe
because your daddy **loves** you so."

"**Superhero Dad,**" I say,
"you are the **best** by miles!"
My dad says,
"I'm no **Superhero,**"
then he stops and smiles . . .

"I know a **Superhero**
who is lots and lots of fun.
Who is it?
Well . . .

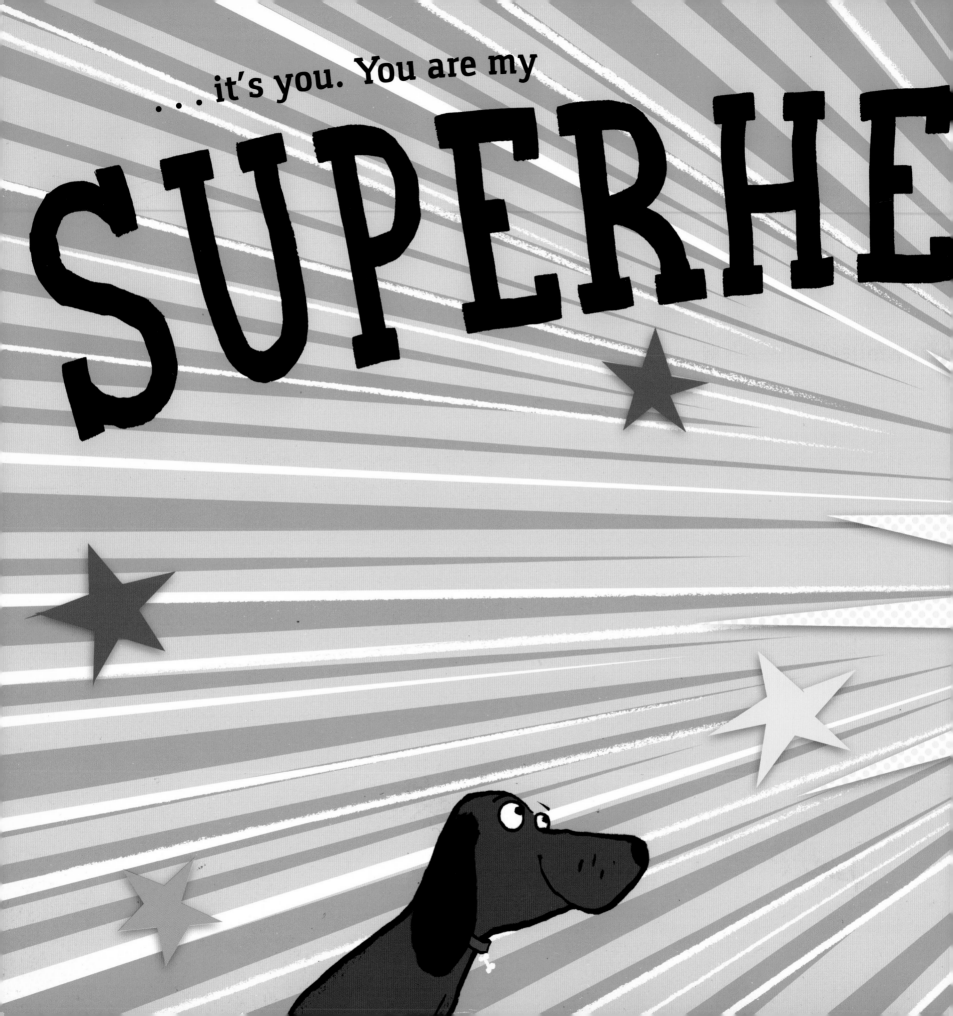

...it's you. You are my

SUPERHE